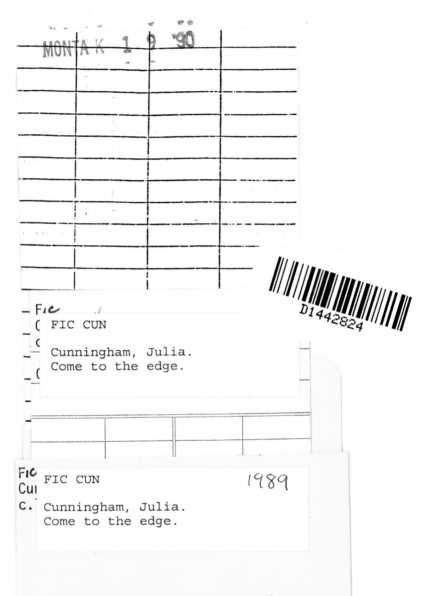

COME
TO THE
EDGE

COME
TO THE
EDGE

Julia Cunningham

PANTHEON BOOKS

Cover art by John Cayea

Library of Congress Cataloging in Publication Data
Cunningham, Julia. Come to the edge.
SUMMARY: After he is befriended by a
sign painter, a confused runaway finds trust and
a purpose for living.
[1. Orphans—Fiction. 2. Runaways—Fiction.
3. Friendship—Fiction] I. Title PZ7.C9167Co
[Fic] 76–44017
0–394–83432–1 0–394–93432–6 lib. bdg.

Manufactured in the United States of America

2 4 6 8 10 9 7 5 3 1

For the beautiful
Mary Ann Larabie
who gave me the morning

Come to the edge.
We might fall.
Come to the edge
It's too high!
And they came
and he pushed
and they flew . . .

CHRISTOPHER LOGUE

CHAPTER

1

Gravel Winter was ten when he was left at the foster farm and those first four years weren't bad. Even the man who headed it, the Principal who had a mouth that never moved when he talked and seemed unable to smile, didn't spoil Gravel's satisfaction in having the same bed in the same dormitory in the same place. No more ugly surprises like waking up in still another grubby room alone, his father drunk in God-knew-what bar where Gravel couldn't find him. He always searched after the second day. It helped obliterate the images of his father's thin, tall body lying dead behind a garbage can or locked up in a cell, his head bloody from a fight. Sometimes he found him. More often he just waited. He was sure of one thing. His father would never desert him, not if he could manage to get back.

He had understood about the farm. His father had explained to him that he wanted to be by himself to make a new start and that he would come for Gravel later. Later had turned into four years, but as Gravel kept telling his friend Skin, that was all right. It just took some people a little longer.

Skin would grin and scratch under the fold of fat that bulged over his belt and ask for more stories about what Gravel had seen, what he had done, because Skin had been at the farm so long he had no memory of anything else.

Gravel couldn't remember a friend before Skin. There hadn't been time or even the chance except for a few words in schoolyards that might have been beginnings but weren't because his father and he moved on before the words could become a base for feelings. And in this place full of people who got adopted or transferred without warning, getting fond of somebody didn't pay off. It could end too abruptly, too soon. But with Skin he had been different. They had talked right off.

It had been a morning in the middle of winter, bright like being blind with the brightness. Skin had started first. "Seen you around ever since you came, been watching you. You don't talk much to anybody."

"Out of the habit," Gravel had replied, surprised at himself for revealing this much.

Skin had laughed. "Not like me. I guess I need words the way a painter needs colors. What do you need?"

Suddenly Gravel had wanted to say, "You, if you don't mind my dumbness," but all that came out was, "Don't know. Never thought about it."

Skin had laughed again, a sound that warmed Gravel. Maybe he wasn't so stupid after all if he amused this person without even trying.

"You will," said Skin. "Give you another week. You know how I see thoughts? Like round, red apples and when you bite into them they juice all over your chin and then you get to the core and spit the seeds down to the ground and they swell into new apples, right there, no waiting."

The boy plucked an invisible shape from the air, polished it on his sleeve and gestured toward Gravel. "Catch!"

Gravel knew he mustn't fumble. He caught the nothing thing and put it in his pants pocket. "For later," he said.

"For later," echoed Skin and turned, smiling, back toward the school building.

Since then they had shared all the moments between meals, classes, and study periods, and Gravel learned a kind of liveliness he had never experienced before. Not only with words but with seeing and hearing. And there was such freedom in their talking that neither one ever, even for an instant, hesitated to speak.

Once Gravel had asked him why he was so fat.

"I don't talk about it but I will to you," the boy had replied. "You're my real friend. The Principal hates fat people and I hate him. I can't annoy him any other way—it would be too dangerous. So I eat like a pig and watch him watching me."

Gravel had laughed and admired this odd person who liked to hear how he had lived, especially about his father.

After lights-out was the best time for the two of them. They'd pretend sleep for about ten minutes and then slip out of their beds and meet in the basement room where the furnace was. Even on bitter nights it was hot down there.

Skin always started. "Must have been okay to have a father around most of the time."

"Yeah, like the afternoon he took me out of that lousy school in New Jersey, had our bags packed and everything, but first we went to a circus."

This was one of Skin's favorites. He always acted as though he, too, had been there, pointing at the acrobats, growling with the lions, eating his popcorn bit by bit because the bag had to last until the end. He knew as clearly as Gravel the exact moment when one of the elephants got out of line in the parade and had to be prodded back, tail to tail with the others, and how the clown in the orange tights had sprained his ankle jumping over a barrel.

Or sometimes, when they both felt quiet, he would ask for the story of when Gravel had the measles.

"You felt punk long before the spots," Skin would begin.

"Long before. Kind of prickly, but I just thought it was mosquitoes or fleas. I didn't get dotted until the morning I woke up and couldn't stand the sun in my eyes. My father took one look at me—he knew—and put down the shades and went for the landlady. They talked awhile outside the door, and then my father came back with a pot of tea and toast with marmalade. For five days he never left me except to get his meals downstairs. And we talked some, too, but not like ordinary days."

"What about?" Skin would ask, though he had memorized the answer.

"About made-up things. My father is great at telling stories. He said he'd read a lot of fairy tales when he was little and had never forgotten one."

"Tell me a couple—like he did."

And so these secret hours passed, Skin living what he had never lived, and Gravel so entwined in these fragments that he sometimes almost believed that if he patched enough pieces together he might magically bring his father back.

The best was rarely requested, just on special nights when one of them had been punished or the meal had been uneatable or when they felt too young to ever get free of the farm.

"He came to see you," Skin would say.

"Three times." And Gravel would reweave those brief, awkward visits where the two of them sat in the stiffness of the reception room trying to think up things to talk about, reweave them into intervals of hugs and confidences and the joyful relief of being together again.

Skin never questioned the truth of what Gravel told him. He was too happy just sharing. And each Saturday he and Gravel would stand at the outer gate and watch the road that led into the world on the chance that Gravel's father might be coming to see him. Usually Gravel's nightmares were worse on Saturday night, but the next morning he had Skin right there ready to listen to the tangled horrors that, after the telling, were no worse than ghost stories out of books. Skin was like a mirror where Gravel saw his real shape. Skin kept the image steady.

So those first four years weren't so bad. But one morning, the sky so dark it seemed like extended night, the thunder pounding as if to shake the earth, the years ended. There was no Skin. Not anywhere. Not in the dormitory, not at breakfast, sitting in the chair Gravel always saved for him, not in the classroom, nowhere.

Gravel broke the first law of the farm, never to disturb the Principal. He left the classroom full of people talking senselessly about the kings of England and ran to the man's private apartment and knocked. He did not wait to be greeted and never even noticed the annoyed surprise that tightened the Principal's mouth.

"Where is my friend?" he said.

"Friend? Who? What are you doing here? My living quarters are off-limits and you know it!"

"My friend Skin—Wally Kemp. He's disappeared."

"He's found a home," was the reply.

"I don't believe you. He'd never have gone without telling me he was going." Gravel seized the edges of the man's jacket and tugged hard. "Where is he?"

With one wide swipe of his right arm the man hit Gravel so forcefully across the face the boy staggered. "You'll be punished for this, you little brat!" His lips parted to show yellowed teeth. He thrust the boy backward. Gravel's shoulders thudded against the door.

"He never!" he shouted. "He never would have gone without me knowing, not if he had to fight to get to me! You've locked him up someplace! Maybe you even killed him!"

"You idiot!" retorted the Principal. "His foster family picked him up before breakfast. Lucky to get a family at his age."

Gravel had no instant of choice. He grabbed for the nearest heavy object—the marble pen-stand on the desk—and struck out at the flesh in front of him, anywhere, anyhow. The Principal caught his arms and held him off until his shouts brought two aides into the room who pinioned Gravel's arms behind him. He tried to fight with his feet. It was only after they had flung him into the small, square room with gray walls that Skin had called the Cell that his body stopped flailing. He huddled into himself, his head against his knees, and just existed.

It must have been the next day when outside the door a certain voice unclamped his arms and raised his head. It was his father. He suddenly ached to be held, to be shut away inside a warmth he could hardly remember. He got to his knees and pressed against the grey door.

Now the voice was the Principal's. "He'll be transferred to a correctional institution if I press charges. But there is an alternative since he is only fourteen. If you take him into your permanent custody."

Gravel rubbed his cheek hard on the grey wood as if he could hollow out a hole to receive his father's answer and let it pour like sweetness into his ear.

The words came like bullets. "I can't. I can't support him. Have a hard enough time making out for myself. He'd be like a stone around my neck. The reason I left him here in the first place. Fact is—" and then it came "—I don't want him."

The rest was obliterated in deafness. Gravel fell away from the door in a kind of faint, though he could still see the single oblong of the window and the dull and sullen sky beyond. Five hours later, the clouds now blackened into night, the terrible emptiness, the descent beyond being lonely, had begun. Its color was grey. Slowly, slowly a terror arose all around him, chilling his skin and jerking at his muscles.

He shoved against it, got to his feet and tried to push it off. But it fitted him too closely. He stared for a moment at the grey walls. Maybe if he got away from them he could free himself. He ran to the window, and with first one foot and then the other he smashed the glass, not caring that the shards sliced through his thick socks and scored his ankles. He worked himself through the opening and dropped to the ground.

He fled.

CHAPTER

2

He crisscrossed three highways and five towns before he decided it was safe to stop. The Principal would never search far or long for him. He came at last to a small stretch of stores and houses by night, by a night that concealed his dirt-stained clothes but whose chill lateness swelled the hunger that was like a knife inside him. One light in one window of one house. He knocked and when the door opened he half fell against a small, compact man whose eyes seemed not to reflect questions. The man pulled him in and led him to a chair.

The rest was diffused, a vague feeling of this person taking off his shoes, of his holding a glass of milk to Gravel's lips and making him drink it, then a long fall onto a bed and into sleep.

The next morning Gravel cleaned himself in the tiny bathroom and came out into the large space that was kitchen and living room together.

The man beckoned Gravel to sit with him at the round table, where a bowl of cold cereal was waiting for him.

"My name's Paynter. Don't laugh. It really is. Didn't choose my profession for me—I'm a sign painter—but it fits very snugly. Yours?"

"I'm a runaway," Gravel replied.

"Guessed that. Was one myself once. Not my business. But I'd like to know your name. Makes things easier. Give me the true one."

"Gravel Winter."

"Yours is as odd as mine. Makes two of us. Want to stay here awhile?"

Gravel nodded, not quite believing the casual welcome of this small, strange man.

"Want to learn something while you're here?"

Again Gravel nodded, consenting as he never had at the farm. They forced. This man asked.

"Eat your breakfast. We'll start easy."

Gravel laid down his spoon, his bowl empty, before the man had taken four mouthfuls.

"Help yourself to more. It's on the counter behind you. I plan on a good dinner tonight. Maybe even lamb chops. That strike you right?"

Gravel nodded hurriedly, not looking up from the cracks that marked the width of the round table. He wanted to get up and leave, but this stranger was being kind. He would at least stick it out until tomorrow.

His cereal eaten, a mug of coffee in his hand, Mr. Paynter got up and led Gravel into the second room. It was large and bare except for a drafting table about twelve feet long at one wall, rows of cans—some filled with paint, others with brushes—two high stools, and a stack of rolls of thick paper leaning into a corner. The man took a broom from the one closet, where Gravel glimpsed a pile of white cardboard, neatly aligned by size.

"This will be your first job in the morning—to give the place a good sweep through. Forget to do it myself most days, so I'll be relieved to hand it over to you to remember. Got to keep my signs clean. Dust never improved them."

"That's an odd smell," said the boy, taking the broom.

Mr. Paynter laughed. "A fragrant blend of gasoline and turpentine. The first for the brushes, the other to thin the paint. You know, it's simple what I do but it needs practice. You'll see."

Before Gravel could open his mouth to tell this man that he wouldn't be staying, he had turned and seated himself on one of the stools and was blocking in a design of letters on a square of flat board. He was so absorbed in what he was doing that Gravel felt alone, alone with the broom. He went into the kitchen-living room and began to stroke up the dust. He went at it slowly, and when in the tiny room where Mr. Paynter slept, he noticed a kind of rhythm in his sweeping. A little like being on a raft with a pole to propel himself down the river.

He went to the doorway of the workroom. "Can I sweep in here now or shall I wait until you're finished?"

"Come ahead. Won't even know you're here. Just watch not to tip the cans. Can't afford a fire. And when you're done, take my wallet from the drawer in the kitchen table and go get us some dinner—the meat and a couple of bargain vegetables to make up for the price of the chops. Ask anybody where to find the market. Only one anyway."

Gravel realized he had been dismissed, put on his own. But why would this person trust him not to steal whatever was in his wallet, go off with it and never come back? It wasn't stupidity, that he knew, but why?

He quietly went on with his job. Mr. Paynter only broke from his lettering once to say cheerfully, "Put some push in that broom. Floor's full of cracks." Once more Gravel became submerged in his thoughts and gradually, like the slow approach of morning light, the swish, swish of the broomstraws took him back to the day he and Skin were set to clean out the loft of the farm's barn. The piles of straw had been removed but the remaining chaff, swirling under their sweeping, caught the sun's first brilliance and surrounded them both in a kind of moving radiance. They had both been aware of the momentary wonder of it.

Gravel's broom struck the floor with a loud slap. He brushed his eyes with his sleeve and swallowed past the lump in his throat. Unconsciously he sniffled.

Mr. Paynter glanced at him and then back to his drawing board. "Not got a cold, have you? No? I get those feelings every now and then, too. Natural. Had a wife once. A brother, too, and a very funny lady cousin who made chocolate creams on Sunday. All gone now. Except they come back when I ask them to. They like to be asked."

Gravel went to the kitchen and scrubbed the few dishes before he took the wallet from the drawer and called out to the man, "I'm going now." Receiving no reply, he let himself out of the house and into the biting autumn of the world outside.

He didn't stay any longer than it took to make the purchases and he found himself hurrying back. He didn't know why, though he told himself it was because it was the only place he had to go to. Later, the meal was a silent hour with only Mr. Paynter's occasional remark, which solicited no response from Gravel. After dinner, he went to his tiny room with his mug of coffee and a book, saying goodnight to the boy before shutting his door.

Gravel washed the dishes, turned out the overhead light, and then sat down at the table. His own weight seemed to pin his body to the chair. The fear was coming again. He tried to barricade himself from it by remembering the flimsy, disconnected moments since his coming to the sign painter's house, but they collapsed before the high sweep of the greyness as it whirled around him, closing in.

"Oh, God!" he called, but his voice made no sound in the room.

Forcing his body upright he went to the mirror that was fastened to a cupboard door and watched his mouth form the "Oh" over again. He had to make certain that he was real, that he had a shape, that he was something more than the despair inside him. The hair he saw was still red, the face still held up by the bones beneath the skin, and when he dared to look straight into his eyes, their deep-socketed brownness was still visible. He stretched his mouth into an imitation smile and was suddenly caught in another cramp of terror.

He bent over the kitchen sink and began to beat the palms of his hands against the steel edges. Gradually the hurting began to become real, and the greyness backed off and away. But it was not until the moon shone blank at the window that he was able to stand erect and move very slowly to his room.

The next day began with the ringing of the phone. After Mr. Paynter had hung up he explained, "A department store job—signs for a sale. I'll be picking up the list this morning and will probably make some calls. I'll be having a beer and a sandwich with somebody or other so you'll be in charge here. Take messages if anyone wants me and help yourself to whatever there is for lunch. You're entitled to some time to yourself, so why not walk around the town at noon? It's a small place but all together. No shopping center, movie house open only on weekends, only three bars. Small, but you know where everything and everyone is and where they'll all be tomorrow."

He shrugged into a worn red and black mackinaw and then paused. "If a very scraggy cat with half an ear comes around, give him some milk. One night about a year ago he meowed my door down. Couldn't stand the crying. He only bothers with me when mice and birds are scarce, but we've learned to respect each other."

He turned the door knob. "You'll be fine," he said and left.

Gravel stood wondering about this unusual person. Was he a drinker? Would he come back at a half-stagger and have to be taken care of like . . . like his father? He tried to plug up the crevices of all those shattered days, to banish the stumbling and the smells, the senseless shouts and mumbles.

At that moment the phone rang. Gravel put the receiver close to his right ear. "Hello?"

"Hello? Paynter there?"

"No, sir. I'm to take the message."

"Must be prospering. Got an answering service. You still there?"

"Yes, sir."

"Tell the artist I'm ready with that rural route of Orangeola signs. My name's Zink. He knows my number. Got all that?"

"I'm writing it down."

"Write it twice. I'm in a hurry to get the job started."

"Yes, sir."

He had no sooner hung up than it rang again. This time it was the post office saying that there was an insured package and would Mr. Paynter come for it.

After he had swept all four rooms, Gravel turned up the collar of his jacket and went out to find the post office. He had only to look down the eight blocks of the main street to sight the flag on the right building. He took his place in line before the one clerk's window, and when he had come to the grill and asked for the sign painter's parcel, the man behind the bars greeted him with a snort.

"How do I know who you are?" he asked. His voice twanged through his nose. "Never saw you before in my life. Don't like the looks of you either. Tell Mr. Paynter to come in himself. Next."

As Gravel reached the street he saw a transparent reflection of himself in the glass front of a shop. His pants bagged, his jacket was streaked with dust and even his red hair was grimy. He looked like someone costumed as a tramp. Why hadn't Mr. Paynter minded, criticized his appearance? Would even Skin recognize him if he passed him in the street? Would he be like the man behind the bars? Had Skin maybe really left the farm without caring whether or not his best friend knew he was going? Had the Principal told the truth?

Suddenly the fear clamped down over his head. He could taste the bile of it in his mouth. He ran, his feet hammering the sidewalk, back to the little house and threw his body onto a kitchen chair and clung with both hands to the edge of the table. It wasn't Skin now. It was his father. And the words, those terrible words booming through the mist that shuttered his eyes. "Fact is, I don't want him."

Gravel had to raise himself up from the drowning greyness. He grabbed the phone and dialed the operator. He had to have a voice in his ears other than the one that was destroying him.

"Hello? Hello? May I help you? Hello?"

He listened avidly but in a moment the voice clicked off. It was then he heard the mewing and the regular scratch, scratch at the front door. He opened it. Anything to push back the fear.

It was the one-eared cat. The animal sniffed at Gravel's legs and then sidled in, circled the kitchen, and looked up at him and meowed again.

Gravel gratefully filled a bowl with milk and then stooped down beside the hungry cat and watched his tongue rapidly lapping up the liquid. He began to breathe more easily, and finally he got up and went to the counter and took out two slices of bread. A little later he was eating a thick cheese sandwich. He and the cat together.

He waited three hours for Mr. Paynter to come back. When he

did, Gravel pretended he hadn't heard the latch click and let the old man speak first.

"Had a pleasurable but very unprofitable day. How about yours?" When Gravel merely shrugged, Mr. Paynter continued. "Something scare you? Look a bit white around the gills, as my grandmother used to say. Any messages?"

Gravel relayed the phone call concerning the rural signs.

"I'm relieved. That's a good contract. Will look it over tomorrow. You can come with me. I'll show you how to fill in the letters. I do the edging."

Before he sat down to supper, the sign painter went to a cabinet and drew out a bottle of red wine with a French label on it. "Ever tasted a fine wine? Well, you're going to tonight. It's an experience no young man should be without." He poured the wine into two jelly glasses and raised his to the boy. "Salute," he said.

Gravel imitated the gesture and sipped cautiously. His father had never offered him even a taste of beer. He felt his insides relax, just slightly. He took two large swallows. The tenseness was even gone from his mind.

"Worth a try, isn't it?" smiled the man. "But don't gulp it all at once. Drink as you eat. Adds savor to the food even if it's canned beans."

Gravel told him about the package and the clerk's refusal to give it to him. Mr. Paynter only nodded and said he'd take care of it.

When they had finished, Mr. Paynter refilled their glasses and leaned forward a little on his elbows. "Now, tell me a few bare facts about yourself. No secrets. They're yours and nobody else's business. Just where you came from."

Gravel started slowly. "I lived on a farm. Did chores, went to school."

"Like any of it?"

15

"Not much, except—" He halted.

"Except what?"

The wine propelled the words. "Except that I had a friend." The silence became a minute.

"What was his name?" asked the painter gently.

Suddenly Gravel wanted to cry, and he knew that if he said Skin's name he would. He shook his head.

"I understand," said the man. "Now let's talk about me."

The tale he told was not long but it bridged Gravel's embarrassment. And he ended the evening by pulling out of a closet a pair of jeans only slightly stained with paint, and a shirt. "You take these," he said. "If I were any bigger they wouldn't fit but luckily I'm not." He handed them to Gravel and said "Goodnight" with a last smile.

CHAPTER

3

The next morning as the two of them set out into the frosted air, Gravel was smiling too. His companion was whistling as they walked and the melody was *"Dixie."* "Helps my legs to get going to give them a marching tune. Want to join me?"

Gravel whistled an octave lower so that Mr. Paynter might not notice that his part was off-key.

So the week began and became two and then three. Gravel graduated to mixing colors and his days became filled with work and learning. First he cleaned out the rooms, as he had that first day, then he washed the brushes—sometimes there were as many as fifteen to be carefully cleansed of the heavy paints—then he wrapped them in precisely folded thicknesses of paper before putting them away in the open cans of gasoline. Answering the phone had become his job whether or not Mr. Paynter was there, and he gradually got to know the regular customers from the new. He made the lunch sandwiches and Mr. Paynter got the dinners.

During his free hour at one o'clock he usually went into town to the little library to read or sometimes just to sit in front of an open book, any book, and look at the people who came in. He had discovered that watching people—doing anything that held his attention—kept his thoughts from the grey country, from the forbidden landscape that was like a kind of continual quaking of the earth underneath him. It was always there—the threat of its return—but out of sight.

And often in the evening, after they had eaten and Mr. Paynter had either gone early to bed or was reading, Gravel took out the box of watercolors he had been given and amused himself by painting little houses and trees and rivers. They were tight and stilted and he always threw them away, but just the doing kept him comfortable.

And all this time the man never forced him to talk or explain.

Then one evening as Mr. Paynter poured their traditional glass of wine, he seemed gayer than usual as though he had been made very happy by some happening.

"Did you get a big job to do?" Gravel asked.

Mr. Paynter's smile became a grin. "No. I just realized, all in a flash, how pleased I am to have company, your company. Makes all the difference."

Gravel lifted his glass to his lips, not knowing how to respond.

"You see, Gravel, I had a brother once. We weren't the same age but might just as well have been. Like twins, the two of us. Did everything together. Even liked to wear the same color sweaters. Know what I mean?"

Gravel gulped and then said it. "Yes. Like my friend and me. Never did tell you his name, did I?" He suddenly had to talk about Skin. It seemed to ease the loss. "Was Skin, or that's what I called him because he really was fat. He liked it. Said that one day he would be skinny when he got off the farm. You see, the farm wasn't what I told you, a regular place for crops and things. It was a kind of orphanage where they put you if there wasn't any other place for you." He was approaching a dangerous boundary and stopped talking.

"What happened to the two of you?" asked the man. "My brother died. Did Skin?"

"We got separated."

"What happened to your feeling about him?"

Gravel took a deep breath. "He didn't tell me goodbye or even leave a message where he'd gone. Got adopted."

"He couldn't, I'm certain," interposed the painter. "And maybe you left the farm in such a hurry, he might have written and they don't know where to forward your letters. Why don't you find out?"

"I can't. They'd catch me for what I did."

Mr. Paynter waited for the rest but when it didn't come he merely added, "Guessed it was something like that. But about Skin—you have to trust the people you love and who love you. Only way to exist."

A bitterness welled up in Gravel so acid that the wine he had just swallowed gushed into his mouth and he ran to the bathroom and was sick. He did not come back to the kitchen but called goodnight from his room.

So the days passed in this refuge of work and rest and warmth. But one night the goodness of it crashed, and all through the double suffocation of fear and hurt Gravel clung to the sides of his narrow bed, face down, waiting for daylight. He needed to see clearly with his eyes before he left this house.

Now it was morning and Mr. Paynter was saying, "Got you again, has it?"

Gravel couldn't speak. He backed to the door and grasped the knob. He had to escape but he couldn't seem to turn the cold round of metal.

Now the man turned from his drawing board. "It's what I said last night, isn't it?"

Gravel relived the moments of yesterday evening. For the first time in all those weeks, Mr. Paynter hadn't appeared for supper, hadn't phoned. Gravel had not eaten but left everything readied for his return. He had even polished the jelly glasses, superstitiously telling himself that their shining would guide his friend home. But the hours had passed, so slowly, so anxiously that Gravel wished he could stop the kitchen clock from ticking. At first he imagined the old man had been in an accident, but this image faded as he began to become immersed in remembering Skin's going.

Then, just as he was about to dash out into the night to search, the loud and laughing voice of the man had sounded behind the door. "Let me in, boy! Can't seem to dig out my key!"

Gravel had opened the door and Mr. Paynter waltzed in, staggered, and then flopped into a chair with Gravel quick to prop him up before he rolled onto the floor.

"Do this once a year," shouted the painter. "Should have warned you. Sorry. Sort of a shock, I guess. Shock, flock, make a mock," he sang off key. "Plucky, lucky, smucky me!" He laughed so thoroughly his head wobbled.

Almost automatically Gravel half lifted him under his arms and maneuvered him to his bed. He laid him down gently and took off his shoes and his jacket, loosened his shirt collar, and drew the covers up over him. It was a hundred times again the nights before the farm.

And just before Gravel left the room, the painter looked up at him, smiled and said, "You'll have to forgive an old coot like me who loves you like a father."

That had been the start of the greyness. And now it was morning and Mr. Paynter was saying, "You're going, aren't you? This time you're going."

Suddenly Gravel knew he would never live through another

bout of this fear. Right now, standing before the one person who had given him a home and no questions, no requirements, no rules, at this exact moment he knew he would not survive another descent into the terror. And if it could come into this warm and welcome place, he had to leave it. Get out and take his sickness with him.

But he owed this man something, some kind of thanks. But why would he want the kind of gratitude Gravel could offer? He had accepted Mr. Paynter's kindness, had learned enough to do the basic work, to be his assistant, and now he was taking himself off, withdrawing his usefulness. His thanks would be so much trash to this man. He did say, to fill in his shame, "You understand, don't you?"

Mr. Paynter laid down his brush, folded his hands, and looked directly at the tall boy before him whose fiery hair and chalk-white face glowed like a mask in the sodden light of the morning. "I understand very little of anything but I resent nothing. I know that you must leave and that the reasons are your own. I've only two questions to ask and neither need be answered."

Gravel waited.

"Going far?" said the sign painter.

The boy was surprised at the simpleness of the question. Anyone could have said this to him, not caring what the answer was. But it wasn't like this man who never pried or demanded.

"Why?"

"Don't go so far you lose the way."

"And the second one?" Gravel knew he couldn't stay much longer within the circle of this man's concern. The greyness wouldn't let him, and if it came down between the two of them, he could never see Mr. Paynter again.

"If you could be transformed," began the man carefully, slowly, "into anything you wished to be right this minute, what would it be?" Mr. Paynter got up from his work stool and stood as tall as his shortness allowed. "Answer. Say it."

"A rock," Gravel gulped out.

"Then you've got to prod yourself alive. You've got to." He led the boy into the tiny side room where he had slept and put his two folded T-shirts, his one pair of socks, and his underwear into a small sack. He handed Gravel the bundle. "First find yourself a place to sleep, then a way to eat."

Gravel felt himself gently pushed to the front door. He didn't look at him again but he heard Mr. Paynter's last words as clearly as if they had been etched out by a trumpet. "I trust you to come back, Mr. Winter."

CHAPTER
4

The words seemed to shove him into the street and a long distance beyond and gradually he started to see where he was walking.

This was a different highway, and just in front of him was the evening outline of a different town. The sky was still a tumble of clouds, the lack of light obscuring all the rooftops except one —a three-story, gabled brown house right in the center. As Gravel entered the town, the outline dissolved into a street of stores, ordinary buildings of wood and brick. Two churches passed him and three gas stations before his tiredness stopped him. He was at the far edge of the town now. He retraced his way to the middle intersection and stood staring at the red-green changing of the overhead traffic light.

Just beneath his direct line of vision he saw a very thin man with a white cane step into the street. Gravel rubbed at the itching of his eyelids, and for a moment time reversed and he was very young, holding onto the wire fence that encircled the farm, look-ing, looking for the coming of a very thin man who was his father. Skin was there too, but shadowy now. He didn't want Skin too distinct. Every now and then a tiny blade of hope would rise in him if the man coming was boney and had unbrushed brown hair, but it never was the right one. It had been a long time since he had permitted this memory to live again, and now the greyness was only a thought away and his homelessness as real as the cement under his feet.

Suddenly a scream and a shriek of brakes jerked him from his thoughts. The old man was five yards away and a car coming too fast to stop in time. Gravel lunged forward, seized the man's right arm, and pulled him out of danger. The man fell before Gravel could support him.

"Goddamn you, boy!" the man screeched. "I'm not a ghost you can pass through!"

Gravel lifted him to his feet. He said nothing.

"You old fool," said an onlooker, "he saved your life."

"Did he now?" He peered into Gravel's face, so near his rancid breath filled the boy's nose. "Then I owe you."

Gravel tried to free himself of the clawlike hand that gripped his sleeve but the fingers only tightened.

"Don't like owing. You come with me. Don't live more'n a block from here and I could use your strength to get me there."

Gravel could only consent, a prisoner of this almost blind eccentric, and he walked with him until they arrived in front of the very house he had earlier seen rise above the silhouette of the town, brown, high, and three-towered.

"That's mine. Ugly, isn't it? Inherited it from a lot of people, all dead now. Just me and my servant left. Williston, that's the servant, told me not to go out by myself but I get sick of his company, have to have some illusion of independence even if my eyes are mostly no good."

Gravel knew that with only a slight pressure on the man's hand he could release himself, but the sting of this hard pinch in his flesh and the loom of the Victorian mansion that he knew he would enter were somehow welcome.

"You have a home, boy?" the old man was demanding. "Don't look it from what I can see. Your bundle isn't exactly a leather case with your initials on it. Something sort of missing in you. I can sense it. Like you didn't belong to anybody."

"I don't," said Gravel.

"Well, then." With these two words his captor led him up the front steps and through a glass door that had opened as if instructed. Now Gravel could see in the dimness the figure of a massive man whose hand was still on the handle of the door.

"This is Williston," said the man as he brought Gravel into a high-ceilinged room whose walls were bookshelves. "My name's Gant. And yours? Might as well have this nonsense over quickly."

"Winter," said the boy, for a reason unknown to him concealing his first name.

Mr. Gant chuckled and it was not a pleasant sound. "Not a bad title for a stray. I'd guess a lot of your days are winters." He hacked out a laugh at his own joke. "Don't think that's funny, do you, Williston, solemn old stick that you are. Well, things are changing around here. Boy, you can have a room on the third floor for the night. Never go up there myself. In the morning we'll see. No, don't sit down. I'm tired. Williston, show him the servant's staircase. No sense scratching up the polish on the other."

Gravel breathed his relief to be away from this twisted person, but as he faced the servant he wondered which was worse.

The man was glaring at him. Gravel involuntarily stepped back. Was it simply his being there that this man resented so fiercely? There could be no other basis for his hostility. The servant turned abruptly and strode to the back hall where he gestured to a steep, narrow staircase and then disappeared into another corridor.

Gravel passed the second floor without exploring. He was aware of seven doors opening onto the wide landing, but there was an atmosphere of hollowness, of expectancy, that kept him going

25

until he reached the third. Here again the seven doors to seven rooms, all wide open for his choosing. He looked into the first one. A high, carved bed, two round tables with thick legs that ended in what seemed to be lions' paws clutching round balls, a blocked fireplace, and two armchairs upholstered in black. The curtains at the two high windows were dull yellow. He quickly went to the next room. It contained the same stumpy furniture, only the curtains were different, these a deep purple.

When he had briefly inspected all seven he knew he couldn't live, even for one night, in any of them. It was a feeling like being squashed. Where then? Should he just go, look for another sleeping place? But he knew his energy was used up. Then he saw the ladder at the end of the hall. It must lead to the attic.

He clambered to the top, there was no trap door to keep him out, and saw what he wanted. At the far side under an oval window was a bed, what was once a school desk, and a wicker chair. Near the bed was a cedar chest. He lifted up the lid and found three blankets and two striped down pillows. He took them out and spread them over the cot. This was even more comfortable than the farm, though there were no sheets. And best of all was the smell. A close kind of fragrance came from the beams, the trunks, the discarded boxes of books, from the generations of sun-hot days on the roof.

He stretched out on the bed and saw from the window green leaves against blue, and for an instant the colors seemed to take on a permanent brightness in his mind, like a frame of stained glass. Then he shut it away, squeezing his eyelids down and turning his head.

He slept.

CHAPTER
5

The next morning he awoke immediately into his surroundings. What had any of this, the house, the room, the two weird people downstairs, to do with him? His stomach was hurting with hunger and he sat up to ease it.

At that moment there was a shout from below. It was Williston. "Come down here! Right now!"

Gravel took the stairs so quickly he might have been floating. The manservant blocked him at the end of the staircase. He spoke low. "I don't want you here."

"Why? The house seems big enough for twenty more."

"I hate him, you know."

Gravel was startled by the curious, disconnected reply but pretended it was sensible. "Then why do you stay with him?"

"I have to, at least for a while longer." Williston stepped back and with his fingers slyly nipped the back of Gravel's neck as he passed into the library. Gravel winced but did not turn. He had been used to unexpected flicks and pinches at the farm. Until two years ago he had been too small to retaliate against the yard bullies. He remembered the taste of blood in his mouth during that final fight and how his own anger had warmed him. It hadn't happened again.

Mr. Gant's voice cut in. "Didn't think you'd get your shelter for free, did you? No. I've decided to let you stay and in exchange I'll expect your company and your services mornings. I'm rich but I give nothing away. You won't eat here. I'm careful what I spend but the room's yours. You shall lend me your eyes from six to eleven. I'll require you to describe whatever is before you. Agreed?"

Gravel paused.

Mr. Gant misinterpreted his hesitation. "Come to think, maybe I'd better find out if you have any words under that red hair of yours." He grinned maliciously. "Describe me."

"You're dry and thin like kindling," said Gravel. What did he have to lose but an upstairs room? His voice came out cool. "You like to splinter people."

"Not bad!" The old man was showing his pleasure. "I like audacity. But even if you'd been stupid you've actually no choice. You're a beggar, boy, and you'll always be a beggar one way or another."

This stung Gravel as Williston's pinch had not. He said one word, "Tomorrow," and walked out past the two of them, down to the sidewalk. The dirt-filled pocks in the cement seemed suddenly to surface. This ribbon of grey expanded and Gravel was afraid to look to either the left or the right. What if this became true—that the greyness would finally and irrevocably take over? What if he were doomed to walk forever on this scabby track?

For two hours he simply followed his feet, dulling his mind to everything but the motions of his pace. Then a cramp of hunger forced his body forward. He prepared to run to reduce the pain when he was halted so surprisingly he lost his breath. Whatever it was enveloped him in its softness.

It was a woman with smiling eyes surrounded by webs of wrinkles. As she staggered against him, a hand gripping each of his shoulders as it might have the rung of a ladder, she gasped out, "Don't let me fall! I'm crippled enough in the legs without broken bones!"

Gravel braced against her plumpness and pushed upward. She regained her balance.

"I'm sorry," he said.

"Don't be sorry, be helpful." Her voice was a cheerful hum. "My name is Mrs. Prior. I live two blocks from here, and you're going to get me home." She was looking at him now, all of him, from his misshapen shoes, his torn socks, his dusty pants, past the jacket that was too big, and when her glance reached his face she smiled entirely. She patted his cheek. "You've a forlorn look to you. Need fattening, too." She laughed now. "I sound like the witch in the fairy tale, don't I? But no more chatting until we get me back into my armchair. Or at least no more serious chatting. I'm given to talk too much." And all the way, as step by step, Mrs. Prior leaning heavily on Gravel's arm, they slowly moved the brief distance, her voice accompanied them.

By the time they arrived at the small, white house surrounded by a border of orange and scarlet and purple zinnias, Gravel had learned to adapt his walk to her limping. It was almost as though he, too, were lame.

"Here's my purse. Just dip into the left-hand side and you'll find my door key. That's right. The lock turns twice. Oh," she sighed as they came into the square, white-walled living room, "what a blessing a chair is!" She plopped herself down into the nearest one, and Gravel saw that there were flowers everywhere, on her dress, the chairs, the curtains—even the one print on the wall was of roses. "I can tell you like my little house," she went on. "A bit overcrowded but I like things close to me. Sit down, child, take that chair and let me look at you."

Gravel obeyed and found the upholstered softness of it as comfortable as the woman in front of him.

"About the skinniest boy I've ever seen," she continued. "And the palest but maybe that's because your hair's so red. Makes a contrast."

Gravel felt himself taking on the form of the person she was describing as though she were lending him reality.

"I'd guess you were about fourteen though most would take you for older. Not like my dear departed son. He was husky, built like a hero. But I'm hungry, aren't you? Why don't you just go to the kitchen, right through that door there, and make us some sandwiches with whatever you find in the refrigerator. There's cheese and peanut butter—that was my son's favorite—and deviled ham—whatever you fancy. Butter's there too, and the bread box is on the counter by the sink. I'll have one. You have two. Plenty of milk."

Gravel blinked as he entered the bright yellowness of the kitchen. The walls gleamed such a color as the sun had never matched. The refrigerator was festooned with a cluster of magnetic daisies. The table under the two windows was covered with oilcloth patterned in daffodils.

He smiled for the first time since leaving Mr. Paynter. All together, not forgetting the outdoor zinnias, her gathering of flowers seemed to equal her talking and their colors were like tiny responses.

He organized the bread, butter, and cheese on the counter, found two glasses in a cupboard, and filled them with milk.

"The knives are in the drawer in the table!" Mrs. Prior called as if guessing his next move though she couldn't see him.

He drew out the largest and was just about to slice the cheese when the yellowness of the room wavered in front of him and became those moments in the barn, the sunlit chaff rising like tiny, golden birds, and in the center Skin, laughing for joy. Then the image blanked out and Gravel knew without looking that his loneliness was about to cover the corners of this bright kitchen with grey. Soon, if he couldn't control it, it would engulf all the colors, drown the flowers, destroy the whole interior.

He broke off a chunk of the cheese and stuffed it into his mouth. As he chewed, as he tasted, the greyness retreated and then vanished. He made three sandwiches, placed them on two plates, and took them to the table where the milk was already waiting.

Mrs. Prior hobbled into the kitchen and sat opposite him. "You're a quiet one," she said. "Now my son, he was so clumsy around the house you'd think he'd lived in the wilderness. But to see him run and jump and play tennis was a marvel. Couldn't be beaten."

Gravel had finished one sandwich and was halfway into the second.

"Don't gulp your food, son. Enjoy it. I never thought to ask you before but where do you live?"

"I'm staying at Mr. Gant's house. Down the next block."

"Not really? You mean he actually had the heart to take someone in? Does he feed you well? Can't imagine such a thing but miracles are possible."

"No, I only have a room there."

The woman looked at her companion for a long moment. Then she asked, "You a runaway?"

"Not exactly." The sandwiches lumped in his stomach. "I just left where I was."

Mrs. Prior laughed. "You're like someone in one of my mystery books. I read a lot because I can't get around much." She hoisted herself up and lumbered into the living room.

Gravel followed quickly. "What do you want?" he asked. "I'll get it for you." Anything to keep safe.

She sat down. "Just hand me that picture on the mantle and open the window while you're about it. It's stuffy in here." She took the photograph and rubbed her sleeve over it though the glass was already shining. She held it out to Gravel. "He was—a runaway, I mean. Never came back." She fell silent.

"Why wouldn't he come back?" Gravel's own words surprised him. Why had he said this? She might think he cared about her when really she was just another person who wanted something or someone to ease her loneliness and he would do as well as any other.

She seemed unaware of him as she continued. "To me, you mean? Oh, he loved me well enough, or at least as much as the poor boy could love anybody. But you see he couldn't come back. He stole things. He forged my name on checks. Not that I would ever have wanted him punished, but he used other people's names later on, and when they came for him he had gone." She looked out of her remembering at Gravel. The tears that had covered her eyes dissolved. "I wonder why I am telling this to you. I've not talked about him for as long as he's been missing. Only to myself."

"Didn't you ever hear from him?"

Now the tears touched her cheeks and she made no gesture to wipe them off. Her hands, palms upward, lay lax in her lap.

Gravel had to escape. He didn't want feelings anymore, ever, with Skin gone. He got as far as the kitchen before he knew he had to return. He picked up the dish towel from its rack and took it in to her. She held it to her face for a moment, then reappeared smiling a little crookedly.

"Don't know when I've been taken like that. Must be having someone in the house. Sit down, I've something to suggest.

Would you like a job, maybe in exchange for your meals? You could take your breakfast with you the night before—hard-boiled eggs and bread and such like—and come back just before lunch. I eat my supper early, at five-thirty. Like the daylight. And for this you'd be my legs—do my marketing, go to the library, and sometimes get me into the town bus so's I could see the world. What do you say?"

Gravel felt himself nodding his consent. What an oddness was happening, as though there had been certain slots set in a design just for him to slide into. Mr. Gant and now Mrs. Prior. His time was being hired by each of them but—and the thought came sluggishly—it was himself he was handing over, as though by these loans of his eyes and his legs he could keep himself free of the greyness.

CHAPTER

6

He wasn't quite halfway back to the tall, bitter, brown mansion when such a sudden anguish poured into him that he grasped out for the nearest support and clung to it, his eyes closed. Why was everyone—first Mr. Gant and now Mrs. Prior—leaning on him, trusting him at least by tolerating him in their homes, demanding —he dug his palms on the wooden points of the picket fence that held him upright—demanding that he fit into their frames, take over their needs? Since he had lost Skin, since he had heard the last words of his father, he was nothing inside. Couldn't they see it, wasn't it plain to them that he was an emptiness, a gangle of muscle and bone and blood that couldn't even endure its own weakness? What would happen when he finally crumpled? Would it be a spill of invisible entrails like the body of a dog he once saw squashed by a truck? Would he direct his own death? His stomach heaved and he gagged air.

At that instant something long and stringy fell onto his chest. He forced himself to open his eyes, to look. A foot away from his face was the face of someone else, a woman. Her eyes were enormously blue.

"I'm so sorry," she was saying. "I'm so terribly sorry! I didn't mean them to hit you."

Gravel saw now that it was a clutch of weeds that had struck him. He lost control. "What's wrong with you?" he shouted. "What's wrong with everybody? Flinging garbage in people's faces!"

The woman in front of him was smiling, a rather shy but pleased smile as though he were saying poems to her instead of tonguing words like gobbets of spit.

Gravel's voice lowered but it still held anger. "Can't you hear what I'm telling you?"

The woman touched her ears with both hands. "I'm quite deaf, dear," she said. "You seem angry about something. Was it my weeds? Did I startle you?"

Gravel's rage collapsed.

The woman had opened the gate now. "Come in, come in! I never have visitors. My deafness is too hard for most people to put up with. But you sit here on the porch and rest awhile. You're very pale, you know. Quite ghostly, in fact."

He sat down hard on the white, board steps of her porch. His heartbeats still hammered against his ribs, but his relief to have recovered from his faintness had freed him from anything but a longing for an interval of peace. She seated herself just above him in a wicker chair, saying nothing, allowing his gaze to wander the extent of her grassplot garden edged by an orderly regiment of rose bushes. Gravel could catch the scent of the roses now, and he wondered at the close cropped grass. It might have been cut with scissors, each blade level with the next.

Quietly she got up and walked to one of the bushes, drew a cutting knife from her pocket and clipped off a white rose. She returned to sit beside him and then, leaning forward, handed

Gravel the flower. When he did not take it she laid it in his lap.

Still no words, only the tiny, light humming of bees.

He touched the rose with his forefinger. Something drifted up from the bottom of his memory, something as indistinct as the song of the bees. He put the bloom to his cheek. The airy trace allied itself to the fragrance; and a blurred kind of music, the sound of someone singing, came to him from very far away and the distance was time. This was all, but the hearing of it drew a smile from his lips. Then the connection vanished.

"I see that you feel better," the woman began in a low voice, "and I wonder if you would do me a favor. Just once because you'll be leaving soon."

Gravel turned. She was as wilted as the rose on his knee would be in a few hours, but there was the imprint of beauty on her high, delicate forehead, her deep, asking eyes, and in the way her head tilted as she spoke.

"You could make me hear if you talked very loud into my right ear. Would you try? It's been a very long time since I heard a voice, and I think I'd like yours."

Gravel made a tunnel of his hands and said through it, though he didn't care about the answer, "Who are you?"

"I heard that! I heard that clearly!" Her face was alight. "My name is Ethel Ransome and I'm quite alone and not unhappy to be so except that I miss sounds. Would you like to say something else? Anything will do."

"Have you always been deaf?" was all he could invent.

"Almost always. Came on me when I was ten. You see, one forgets the voices of things. Not trains or gongs or explosions. The loud ones are not so easily lost. But the others, like a pillow falling on a carpet or a piano played well or leaves in the wind or even one's own footfalls on a hardwood floor, those things steal away very early and they leave a vacancy behind them because they were friends. But I'm sure you're not interested in all that. You're young and you can hear. But I wonder if you know how to whistle? If you do would you whistle a tune for me? Oh, don't be embarrassed. I guess I shouldn't have asked. But maybe to-morrow? About three? I'll be up from my nap then and we'll talk some more." Her eyes laughed. "And I promise not to request any whistling."

She rose from the step and went into the house.

Gravel hastily got up and called to her, "But I won't be back!"

It was obvious from the serenity of her expression as she turned that she hadn't heard him. Her words confirmed it. "At three then. I'll look forward to it." She paused as she watched him pick up the fallen rose. "You're a good person. I can tell. Goodbye." The door closed behind her.

Gravel kicked the weeds all the way down to the corner. What did they want of him? And why him? Insulated in his thoughts he wandered slowly back to the Gant mansion. It was not until he was up in the attic, having been let in begrudgingly by the grim manservant, that another fierce wave of anger fired up in him. He stood as strict as a column as it licked at him from his heels up over his legs and torso and finally mounted around his head like a crown of flames. He existed only in the volcanic heat of this fury.

It left him as swiftly as it had come. For an instant he expected to fall into ashes, to disappear forever. He rubbed his arms against his sides. He was still encased in his own skin. He scrubbed his fingers through his hair. It was as thick and tangled to his touch as before. He inhaled. There was no pain in his lungs. He was whole.

Next he glanced hesitantly into a corner of the musty room, then into the eaves of the ceiling. The fear, the old fear of the greyness, was crouched in the black crevices of the beams like an

37

eager rat. He knew what the explosion of rage had taught him. He must take a stand. He must decide something that would force the emptiness to leave him.

Three images entered his mind, Gant, Mrs. Prior, and Ethel Ransome. They were all he had to use. He lined them up in front of him and spoke. "You want me, you can have me! I'll throw away whatever there is left of Gravel Winter and move and eat and talk and see for you, just for you. You've each begged a piece of me, go ahead and take it! And I'll fill myself up with you even if I choke on you and, by God, you will want me for it!"

He flung himself down on the cot and fell into sleep like a stone.

CHAPTER

7

Though he had had no dinner and there was no breakfast in view, when Gravel awoke the next morning he was not hungry. He was, on the contrary, curiously filled, as though he had feasted on and off all night. There was also a new kind of lightness, a buoyancy, in him as he descended to the bathroom on the floor below. First he took a bath, scrubbing himself pink with the back-brush that hung on the wall. Then he washed his hair and slicked it flat to his head. Next he washed his extra pair of socks, his other T-shirt, and his shorts, and laid them out on the old-fashioned spines of the radiator. Back in the attic he finished dressing, and as though it were habitual instead of a dread, he looked at himself in the mirror over the chest. He smiled slightly, pleased at his neatness, and stopped to wonder why, for the first time in his life, he cared. Then quickly he fled from the thought. It had cost him a twinge of discomfort.

Quietly, in case anyone were still sleeping, he walked down to the second landing. Just below he heard voices and then saw Williston leading Mr. Gant into the library.

"You can leave me until lunch," the old man was saying. "I can pass up your gloomy company now that the boy's here to read to me and tell me what he sees. He may be a complete idiot but at least it will be a change. Get him."

"I'm coming!" Gravel called, but he hadn't reached the bottom step when Williston blocked him to a halt.

He spoke in a hiss, very low. "The old man wants you. All polished up, aren't we? Different from yesterday. Not that he'll notice so you've done it for nothing."

Gravel tried to push him aside but the man was as solid as a concrete post. "Not done yet, boy." The glint in his eyes made Gravel look away. "Come to oust me, haven't you? Planned it out careful, pretending to be a lost child, a thing to be pitied. Well, we'll see who wins this little game, you or me."

The boy smiled as if no words at all had been built between them.

Williston sneered. "No use wasting that on me. I've my own plans and they don't include you. Now get in there!" He shoved Gravel forward but Mr. Gant did not see his stumbling entrance. He was seated in a leather wing-chair directly facing the curtained windows, as though just being there would make it possible for him to see the full view of the street.

"Good morning, sir," said Gravel. "Did you sleep well?"

The man laughed dryly. "Swallowed a nightingale, did you? Very nice. Thought yesterday you might be dumb."

Gravel went to the windows and pulled the drapes aside. "It's very dark in here, sir, and outside the sun is clear." He gazed a moment at the two rows of houses, all shrunk to smallness by the size of this one mansion. The lawns were clipped, the street as though freshly washed down, but no people. "There's a scatter of birds eating seeds from a hedge."

Mr. Gant was listening and the meanness left his voice. "That so? What else?"

For a second Gravel thought of inventing passers-by to entertain this sour person who now owned part of himself, but just as he was about to begin a woman came slowly toward them up the sidewalk.

"There's a thin lady going somewhere with a basket over her arm and she seems to be talking to herself. Has a dark blue hat on the top of her head like a little round pie and her basket is empty, so she must be heading for a grocery store."

Mr. Gant grunted approvingly. "Very observant, have to admit it. That would be Miss Ethel Ransome. Deaf as a log. Never had much, her people were poor. Don't know as I ever saw her at a party. Has one virtue, however. Doesn't gossip." Mr. Gant nudged Gravel with his elbow. "Can't hear it to pass it on! Get the joke, boy?"

Gravel flinched but not at the poke in his side. He remembered his own unheard yelling at her. But he would make it up to her. After all, she shared him now.

The old man hadn't remarked his inattention. "Some said she was beautiful once but this town likes to romanticize things. Rumor is I'm so rich my cellar's filled with treasures. Nothing down there but coal and potatoes. Say I'm a miser, too."

"Are you?"

Mr. Gant laughed and this time it was real amusement. "Possibly, possibly. Doesn't do to admit a fault, however. Remember that, boy. Williston believes these things. Been trying to rob me for years, but except for what he can squeeze out of the household accounts, he's not found a fortune. What else do you see?"

"A cat crossing over."

"Anything after it?"

"No. Would you like me to read to you, sir?"

"Not a bad idea. Like to hear a page or two of the dictionary. Should be right there on the desk. Start with the g's. My vocabulary gets rusty just talking to Williston."

41

Gravel obeyed but soon came to words he couldn't pronounce. Mr. Gant mocked him by imitating his mistakes, his face quick with pleasure. When he had tired of this game he stood up. "All right, that's enough comedy for one morning. You can take me around the back garden now."

What Gravel saw as they sat down together on a stone bench just behind the neglected conservatory at the rear of the house was a ruin. The paths of slate blocks were cracked and tumbled upward by errant roots. The grape arbor at the far end was a twisted thicket of dead vines. The rose bushes were deformed and had tangled themselves into the high nests of weeds and grasses. Even the trees, though still leafy, seemed prematurely aged, their sap too strained to nourish them. Piles of rot cloaked their roots. Of what must have once been borders, thick with flowers, only an infrequent morning glory showed a few blooms, and through the entire spread of the place was the faint rustle of dryness, of abandonment.

"Well, boy?" asked the old man impatiently. "How is it flourishing? Count the roses for me. And what of the vegetable garden? See any corn?"

Gravel couldn't even imagine where the vegetables might once have been planted. Then he relaxed and began like a kind of song. "Of roses there are pink ones, red ones and, far off, crimson. No yellows yet. The marguerites are white beyond the zinnias and—"

Mr. Gant put his hand on the boy's arm. "Let's go back." He said nothing further until they were once more in the library. "You may go for the day now, boy." He paused, his hands clasped tightly together. "That's the way it once was, my garden. Thank you. Now go."

CHAPTER

8

Gravel did not need to knock at Mrs. Prior's door. It was open. He heard her oven slam shut and then her voice. "Come in, child. I'm baking some muffins. This first time you're company." But as he went into the kitchen he saw her hurriedly setting a second place at the table and knew she hadn't been certain he would come.

"Milk or cocoa? My son could never quite decide so I'd choose for him."

"Choose for me then."

Her plump face curled with smiling. She started to lift a casserole from the stove.

"You sit down, Mrs. Prior, and let me serve."

"That's thoughtful of you, child. I accept. My legs are full of aches today."

The bubbling pot smelled of herbs as Gravel placed it on a mat in the center of the table. He was suddenly so hungry it was difficult for him to watch Mrs. Prior spoon out the meat and carrot chunks onto his plate. He had forked a piece of meat into his mouth before she had completely served herself. He hastily put down his fork.

"Go right ahead. We had a rule in my family—there were twelve of us, counting my aunt—that food was meant to be eaten hot."

Gravel recognized this as kindness. But why? He was one day away from being a stranger to her. Suppose he had never happened by. Would she have taken in just anybody?

Gravel bent to his meal and ate through it without speaking.

"You can take what's left of the muffins for your tomorrow's breakfast," she commented as they finished with a bowl of stewed peaches. "You look better, more color in your cheeks. Is it not too depressing at Mr. Gant's?"

"No, it's fine," Gravel answered, avoiding any speech that might connect this house with the other. He had to keep them separate and didn't know why. He got up and cleared the table, taking the plates to the sink and turning on the hot water.

"That's good of you," said the woman. "I'll go sit on the porch and you join me when you've finished."

He lingered over the small job, wishing he could tell himself why he had resisted talking about Mr. Gant, and he knew, too, that he would never carry over anything from one house to the other as if, in giving himself away, it must be done piecemeal.

He dried the last glass and went out to sit beside Mrs. Prior.

"You're thoughtful," she said gently.

Gravel was not embarrassed. Before he might have been, but now he felt a kind of satisfaction cover him. He was gaining over the greyness so fast he could now almost see himself, his actions, as graceful instead of angular. He glanced down at his worn pants and they seemed momentarily unfamiliar.

"Also one could depend on you, not like—" she let the sentence break, but Gravel knew she meant her son.

"Yes," said the boy gravely, beginning to believe his actor's role was true, "you can depend on me." The lies behind it were dwindling out of sight.

"Would you have time to go for some groceries this afternoon? Oh, I'm sure you have other projects more fascinating than shopping for me, but I do need potatoes and butter and milk and you can get a treat for yourself. You could stop by with them anytime just so's I'll have an hour to get our supper cooked."

"If I'm back in a couple of hours, would that be all right?" Gravel had remembered his promise to Miss Ethel.

"Just fine. But go into the house first and look in the hall closet. I've saved all my son's clothes, and some of them will fit you. Better maybe when I've added a bit of fat to your bones but go and see."

As he opened the door on the array of cellophane-covered suits and pants and jackets the odor of moth balls spread out from them. A memory cut into him, a happening so long past he knew he must have been very young. He had fallen into a trunk so high he couldn't get out. It was empty except for the stifling smell of moth balls and his fear had believed it to be his coffin. He remembered screaming until someone had come and as he was lifted out someone had kissed him.

"What's the matter?" called Mrs. Prior. "Take your choice, try them on."

He guided his hand to a grey jacket and then quickly drew out the next. It was blue. Farther along the rod hung a pair of black corduroy pants. He chose them. He looked at his own shirt and knew it would never be really white again. Among those of the dead man he found another white one with a red arrow down the front. He turned to Mrs. Prior. "Will it be okay if I take these?"

She smiled. "Of course. Now go put them on. Leave your own clothes and I'll see what I can do with them. If they're too far gone I'll discard them. You'll just have to use what's left in the closet."

He went into the privacy of the living room and made the exchange. The storage smell was dissipating. He placed himself before the long mirror on the wall. Except for the narrow face and red hair, he might have been greeting a stranger. He tried a smile. It blazed above the red arrow in sudden unfamiliarity. Maybe he had really become the new person, the one who was learning to be what was wanted.

He joined Mrs. Prior on the porch and presented himself.

"How handsome you look!" she exclaimed. "Even seem to have added more width to you." But her eyes were saddened. Then she beckoned to him. "Come nearer, child."

He advanced two steps but no farther.

Painfully she got to her feet and closed the distance. She took hold of the jacket collar and straightened it. Then, like the touch of a wing on his right cheek, he felt her lips leave a light kiss.

He jerked backward.

She pretended to ignore his rejection. "It's just so good to have you sharing his things! I can't get over it."

He knew what she wished. He knew what she expected. He knew what she was waiting for. All right, he would play it to the hilt. He leaned down and kissed her. She smelled like face powder and violets.

She hugged him and he forced himself to stay still, but something inside, at the center of him, wanted to run.

CHAPTER

When he arrived at the market he stopped in the passageway of canned vegetables, high as a hedge, and looked idly at the sale signs. Beans were the week's bargain. The printing of the prices was crudely, hurriedly done, and Gravel brushed imaginary numbers over them, correcting the lines; and as he did it he saw in his mind Mr. Paynter bent over his drawing table, his right hand steadily recreating the alphabet. How sure and right his letters always were. Why couldn't he have stayed there, apprenticed to a future instead of trading pieces of himself in exchange for food and a place to sleep? But before the answer flashed back at him, before he could fully remember the engulfing greyness, he drew Mrs. Prior's list from his pocket and began to hunt out the items.

Her requests completed, he remembered that she had told him to pick out something for himself. He knew she would be hurt if he didn't, so he inspected the rows of bagged candies. Not these. The chocolate bars were piled up by sizes. He selected the medium one and wheeled his cart to the nearest checker. Later, the bag in his arms, the change from the purchase carefully deposited in an empty pocket, he left the noise and glare of the store.

Outside he immediately wished he were back inside it.

Clouds had surfaced the sky and Gravel tried to reason his way past his uneasiness. He began to pretend he was going to buy a house and he inspected each one as it confronted him. At first he considered the larger ones with generous windows and kept gardens, but as he walked one block after the other, his choices were becoming smaller and smaller. There would be less space in these for echoes, for shadows. But no matter how little, how cramped, there he would be, trapped inside and alone. He discarded the game and rubbed his free hand down the side of his leg until his palm tingled against the ridges of the corduroy. He shifted the package of groceries and looked around to see where he had come.

Just then a voice called to him. "Young man! I knew you wouldn't forget me! Come right in!" It was Ethel Ransome.

"But I did," Gravel murmured.

"I'm fine, thank you," she continued. "Good of you to ask." She opened the gate for him. "Put your parcel in the house and then you can help me weed the beans. In the back. They need attention, poor things." She led him through the house, not looking to see if he were following.

The ceilings were low, the living room and what he glimpsed of the bedroom were stuffed with furniture, decreasing even the basic smallness. A kitchen completed the space. Gravel felt that if he stretched his arms and waved them the whole house might tumble. He smiled as she turned to him, now bending over a stand of beans, and she smiled back at him. "Oh, this is fun!" she said. "Now you take that end of the row and I'll take this and soon we'll meet in the middle."

"Where did you get your new clothes?" she called in a loud voice though they were only five yards apart.

Gravel went to her and talked directly into her ear. "A friend gave them to me." He returned to his weeding.

"What a lovely voice you have. Very resonant. You said a friend. You must have lots of them, handsome and kind as you are. I used to." Her words continued, filling the sunlit air like dust motes, and Gravel paid as little attention to them. He knew from the hum of them that she was happy.

When they had finished and he had dumped the weeds in the compost heap, she ushered him back into the house, plumped up the cushions on the sofa in the living room, and sat down, patting the place beside her. She had picked up a wide photograph album, and as he joined her she spread it across their laps.

One after the other the faded faces appeared and vanished with the turning of the pages. The names, too, were old—Abigail, Grace, Percy, Magruder, Mary-Faith, Jameson. Like a film these people, existing only for her, and accompanying them Miss Ethel's memories and anecdotes and surmises, wreathing them with a moment of life.

Halfway through she stopped. "But you're not getting a chance to say anything at all! I'm ashamed. My manners seem to have left me. Tell me about yourself. Go ahead, don't be shy." She shut the album and rested one hand on his shoulder as if to assure him of her interest. When he didn't speak she added, "Make it up, if you like. I won't know the difference and it will give me so much to think about later."

Gravel swallowed his reluctance. Hadn't he decided to fill up the hollows of himself, create a new person? He had already impressed his willingness, however false, on Mr. Gant and Mrs. Prior. Why should he hold back from this lonely little deaf lady who, after all, was only asking to hear his voice?

He began. "I wasn't much to start with, just a baby." Her

trickle of laughter encouraged him. "But I soon realized that I had been born into a very special kind of house. It was a castle. A castle with towers, four of them, a courtyard as big as a park, and five automobiles garaged where the ancient stables had been."

"Do go on! What was the inside like? As you came in, I mean."

From there it was easy. The invention of tapestry and gold plate, of servants and feasts, of fox hunts and dances, all out of books, and before long Miss Ethel was contributing to the game, adding the colors of the costumes, the string orchestra that played only waltzes, the kinds of horses, and of course, the rare dishes that emerged from the palace kitchens.

It was only the lowering of the sunlight at the windows that reminded Gravel he had yet to deliver the food to Mrs. Prior. He got up. "And that was it," he said, halting them both.

Miss Ethel laughed. "What a glorious afternoon! I feel quite as young as when we lived in our castle!"

Gravel looked at her and saw again that faint flash of what had truly once been beauty. "I have a present for you," he said and drew the now lumpily warm chocolate bar from his pocket.

He turned his back on her surprised delight. He didn't want to witness her gratitude for something he gave without any love behind it. As for the temporary pleasure of the castle game, well, that was just a play of lies.

He waved as he regained the sidewalk but did not look toward her. If she were content with their foolishness so much the better, and maybe what they had imagined was more real than what was walking down this particular street, dressed like a human, carrying a stranger's supper to her.

CHAPTER
10

So the days passed into late summer. Gravel's schedule of attending to Mr. Gant in the mornings, taking his meals with Mrs. Prior, and providing a listener for Miss Ethel grew like a kind of cocoon around him. It was both a soft and temperate climate of living, a welcome kind of nearsightedness where he almost never had to cope with anything that might have struck or stung him, shut off as he chose to be. Only once was he forced to avoid a jolt—one afternoon when leaving the market he thought he saw Mr. Paynter coming toward him. This older man had been smiling mildly at nothing in particular, as though he were content with merely the shafts of sun and shade that bannered the sidewalk. It was someone else but the likeness was so close Gravel had for one sharp instant wanted to call out to this stranger.

It was that same afternoon, after he and Mrs. Prior had finished lunch and he had washed the dishes, that she proposed a future for him. "I hope you don't think I'm a busybody," she said, "but you should soon be thinking of what you want to be in life. Now my son would have been better off with a career in the Army. Good discipline, no worries about where he slept or ate, and an occupation. But he only changed the subject whenever I suggested it. Poor child, he couldn't see beyond his pleasures and the money he had to have to buy them. But you, you're different."

Gravel had managed to lead her away from the idea by saying he had promised to go early to Miss Ransome's, that she had asked him to wash her windows, and he excused himself immediately.

But he was not to finish the day peacefully, for even Miss Ethel had decided to voice her notion of his tomorrows. He was scrubbing the top shelves of her kitchen cabinets, three rungs up on a ladder, when she started, her words floating up to him like gnats.

"You know, I think of you a great deal when I'm awakened at night by a dream or when I've nothing to do but sit, and I've something to propose to you. If you don't want to go back to school, why not learn a trade, a good trade like being a locksmith or a carpenter?" Her tone was hurried and nervous. "You could live here until you were earning and I'd never interfere with you. Oh, if you're thinking the house is too small for the two of us, I'd planned to give you the bedroom. I'd fix up the back porch, screen it in, and put up glass windows. It would make a very tidy bedroom for someone as little as I am."

Gravel sprinkled cleanser over the already washed shelf. If he made his silence long enough, maybe she would back down.

"You go right ahead and finish up there. I know you can't answer until you can talk right into my deaf old ear."

Gravel turned and shook his head, refusing while he was still out of reach of the plea he knew would be in her eyes.

He saw her shrug and a moment later she left the room. When the job was done, he only paused long enough to shout goodbye before he hurried off.

But he was not to dodge the last loop of the rope that sought to circle him, for that very evening Mr. Gant broke his custom of never seeing Gravel except in the morning, and as he passed the library the door was open and the old man waiting.

"Come in for exactly three minutes," he instructed the boy. "Don't sit down. Just attend to what I am going to say. I've connections in this town, good ones. People owe me favors I've never collected. Now listen, boy. I can get you a position as a clerk in the bank and you can work your own way up. I'll use my influence only to find you a stool to sit on. After that it's your responsibility what happens. Grateful, are you? Speak up!"

"Thank you but no, sir." The words came out unnaturally loud.

Mr. Gant grunted. "All right, that's that. Won't mention it again. Goodnight."

As Gravel went slowly up the three flights of stairs, he felt that the evening dusk that blued the landings was not just the usual darkening of the day but was cueing in the end of summer. The next morning, as if he had guessed the truth, the attic roof was being pelted with rain.

There was such a lessening of light that Gravel had to grope for his shoes. He tried to keep the enclosing gloom at bay by turning on the one lamp and then stuffing the orange and the roll Mrs. Prior had given him for breakfast into his mouth in oversize pieces as he dressed. His breath seemed to have thickened in his lungs. He looked around the slant-ceilinged room. There was nothing, no object in it that was his own. It could have been the habitation of a ghost. No book, not even a postcard he might have chosen for the landscape on it. Nothing. Only the slightly damp smell of his clothing and the tumble of blankets on his bed told of his presence. Why hadn't he added something, anything of himself? His uneasiness increased and now he stood, his back to the window that was opaque with the slashing of the rain, ready to bolt to anywhere.

The yelling broke his tension. "What in hell are you doing in the basement? Williston, come up out of there! I've been waiting for my tea a good half-hour!" Then, even wilder, "Boy! Get yourself down here on the double!"

Gravel leaped down the stairs, two at a time, and lunged into the library. Mr. Gant's face was mottled with anger. "That fool thinks I don't know what he's up to! Has no business in the cellar unless I send him there. You go see what's what. I'd never make the first five steps without falling." The anticipation threw his body into a kind of jig that cast a jerking shadow onto the far wall.

Gravel waited no longer. He cut across the grotesque silhouette and a moment later was carefully descending the steep cellar staircase. At the bottom was a wide square of flooring lighted by a single bulb and three doorways cut into the walls like black oblongs. He did not call the servant's name but instead peered into the first darkness. The smell of coaldust met him. The underground room was almost completely filled with heaps of coal, leaving no space for anything else. He tried the next one. Here he could barely perceive that the floor was of hard-packed dirt. On three sides were shelves containing huge sacks of what were probably potatoes and other stored foods. Empty wine racks leaned against the fourth wall.

Williston must be in the third room. Gravel stuck his head inside and said, very low, "Williston, are you in there?" No reply. He entered. On a pile of sacking, not far from the gigantic furnace, lay the long, powerful figure of the man. He was snoring. Gravel leaned down to touch him awake and noticed that his hands were brown with dirt, his fingernails clogged with it.

"Williston," he repeated, poking his arm. "Wake up. Mr. Gant needs you."

The man's eyes opened blearily. He said, almost in a growl,

"What the devil do you want with me?" and hoisted himself heavily to his feet.

"I told you. Mr. Gant sent me to find you."

Now they could both hear through the floorboards the high screech of the old man's scolding but not the words.

"None of your damned business where I am. I was tired. Couldn't get to sleep upstairs."

Why would this man, who had never bothered with him before except to sneer, explain his actions to him? And who would abandon the ease of a bed in a heated room for this dank place? But Gravel didn't dare question him. There was too much menace in him.

Williston led the way upstairs. He stood before Mr. Gant, his hands behind his back, and impassively let the old man's words pelt him.

"You a kind of monster who chooses a cellar for sleeping instead of your more than adequate bedroom? I can tell by your usual sullenness that I'm not about to receive any kind of proper reply or reason, so get yourself into that kitchen and make my breakfast. Right now!"

He turned to Gravel. "Since you're here you can sit with me while I eat. Want some coffee—that is, when he chooses to bring it?"

Gravel nodded. Any company, any place was better than none, better than his hollow attic room on this day of rain and the creep of loneliness.

CHAPTER
11

Two hours later Gravel was knocking at Mrs. Prior's door to no response. Three times, until he was pounding. Still no stir, no sound from the interior. He hurried to the back, the rain on his cheeks like hands wiping themselves on his skin. The door was off the latch.

"Mrs. Prior!" he called from the kitchen.

"Upstairs, child!"

She was in bed, a rose quilt up to her chin, her face pale. "Felt too achey to get up. Starting to mold around the edges, I guess."

"I'll bring you something to eat," said Gravel. He didn't want to feel sorry for this woman. That would somehow spoil the role he was trying to fit into. It must all be done—the thoughtfulness, the fetching and carrying—deliberately, not from impulse.

In ten minutes he had set a tray with toast, a boiled egg, and a pot of tea.

"You're a dear soul," Mrs. Prior sighed, pushing to a sitting position against the pillows. She bit into the toast hungrily. "You must feed yourself, too, you know. There's ice cream to finish and plenty of cheese. But then you know my housekeeping now as well as I do, maybe better. Oh, and would you mind just giving the house a sweep through? I've not felt up to it all week. No—don't go yet. I've something else to say." She put down her cup and looked at him almost solemnly. "You don't know what you mean to me. Not because of all the things you do for me, but because of your being here, because of yourself."

Gravel wondered if his face were as red as his hair. He mumbled what he hoped sounded like a thank-you and left her, grateful that she had given him an excuse to go; and as he started to sweep the living-room carpeting, he wondered also if he looked in the mirror on the wall would he have a different face, be perfectly handsome. Maybe what the woman said was true. Maybe he had truly changed; by acting out her image of himself he might have slipped into it. He was for the first time that day unaware of the rush and drip of the water pouring from the roof gutters, of the little squalls of the wind.

When he had completed the sweeping and the dusting and made sandwiches for both of them, he heard the stairs creak and saw Mrs. Prior coming cautiously down.

"Decided it was lonely up there. No, you needn't help me. Like the tortoise I'll win the race, but slowly."

Gravel was just pouring himself a glass of milk when they both heard a tiny scratching at the kitchen door.

"Let it in. Can't be a rat."

The boy obeyed and a grey length of drenched fur hurtled across the floor and under the table.

"My word!" exclaimed Mrs. Prior. "A cat! Can't have it here. It would tangle itself in my legs and make me fall. But give it some milk and a chance to dry out."

Though Gravel would just as soon not have been befriended by the boney, lost animal, it chose his lap to sit on while it tongued its fur clean.

"You see," said Mrs. Prior from her wing chair, "liking you is instinctive. Felt it myself from the first time I saw you. Before you go you'd best take my son's raincoat from the closet. This downpour looks like all day. And you're going to have to take that cat with you."

There was no protest, no unsheathing of claws, when an hour later Gravel gingerly tucked the cat under the raincoat, holding it to his chest with one hand.

"Goodbye, dear!" Mrs. Prior called from the porch. "Why not keep it yourself?"

Gravel was tempted, as he turned the first corner on his route to Miss Ransome's, simply to dump the animal, but the drive of the rain against his own legs, the sting of it on his face, blocked the action. He ran the last three streets and dashed onto the shelter of Miss Ethel's tiny porch before he released the cat.

Like a repetition of his arrival at Mrs. Prior's, no one answered his knocking. Was he late or early? Always before she had been ready at the other side, waiting for him. He turned the knob. The door opened. He didn't notice the cat slipping inside in front of him.

The curtains were still drawn in the miniature living room and the objects in it were nearly invisible. But from where he knew her rocker was he heard the whop, whop of the chair in motion. Now he could dimly make out Miss Ethel herself tipping back and forth, her eyes squeezed shut.

"Miss Ethel," he said into her left ear, tapping her on the shoulder at the same time so as not to startle her. "It's Gravel. What's the matter?"

She looked at him but the usual leap of a smile when she greeted him was absent. "It's this terrible dreariness. Makes things worse."

The light varnish of confidence, even falsely applied, that he had felt at Mrs. Prior's began to melt. Why was this assumed role of helpfulness, of service, so difficult? What could he do now to keep his new image solid?

The cat took over. It sprang into the woman's lap and nudged its nose against her limp hands. Tentatively she stroked it with her fingertips, and when she felt the purring vibrate on her palm, she finally smiled. "It's talking to me," she said and lifted it to her right ear. "No. Can't quite get it." At that instant the cat meowed and Miss Ethel laughed aloud.

She really saw Gravel now. "It's very dark in here, dear. Do open the curtains. Is this your cat? Very skinny, isn't it?" The animal was now sniffing at her neck, its whiskers tickling her chin.

Gravel leaned down. "I brought it to you."

"To me? A real present? Oh, how very kind you are! Haven't had a present since I was young enough to have birthdays. Couldn't do without you, you know."

Gravel's throat suddenly clenched, as though someone or something were choking him. His head throbbed. Why wasn't he pleased to have so fully deceived this old woman back into contentment, into a conviction that he was someone who loved her?

"I have to go now," he shouted at her. The water that dripped down the sleeves of his new raincoat was icy between his fingers.

"Of course, dear. I'm sure you must. Boys are busy creatures. Tomorrow then?"

She didn't wait to observe if he replied but bent her head to hum a small tune to the cat.

Gravel re-entered the rain and walked directionless, slowly, as if he had suddenly gained twenty pounds, until it was time to return to Mrs. Prior's.

CHAPTER
12

Their supper together was silent though Mrs. Prior's mouth was curved at the corners as if she had a secret.

Gravel ate hastily, wanting the meal to be over. But after he had cleared off the dinner plates and set out the two cups of coffee, she spoke. "Now, child, if you will look in the bread box you'll find a surprise. Lift it out carefully. The frosting might slide."

It was a cake, white with little squirts of pink that might have been flowers, and printed in the same wobbly lines, "Happy Birthday to Gravel."

"But it isn't my birthday!" The words burst out of him explosively.

Mrs. Prior didn't seem to hear the tension in his voice. "Of course not, but I just wanted to celebrate it today for some reason. Well, I do have my reasons but that's for later. When is your birthday, child?"

"I don't know." He had to lie, he couldn't give that first day of October to anyone because once his birthday had really happened. It had been before the foster farm and all he had left of it was blowing on a cake with candles and feeling someone's arms around him and that same person kissing his ear. The others hadn't counted.

"Needn't tell if you don't want to," Mrs. Prior was saying. "But you can eat it. Go on. The first slice belongs to you."

Gravel managed two pieces to make up for his bluntness, but the sweet richness rested like lumps in his stomach. He made himself listen to this woman's talk. The words pattered in his head like rain dropping.

"I've some savings. Intended them for my son but, well, you know all about that. I've decided to give part of them to you so you can go back to school and be somebody. Not that you're not somebody already, but you need schooling to succeed in life, need to be just ahead of the ones around you so you can step to the front."

A groan rose to his mouth but he suppressed it. "I don't want your money. You don't even know me."

"I do, dear, I do. You've proved yourself kind and thoughtful and willing to be leaned on by a lame old lady and that's what I call loving her."

Gravel got up abruptly, using the putting away of the cake as an excuse for turning his back on her. His whole body shuddered as he willed it still. If he could only shed these clothes that had once been her son's and step back into the old, soiled ones she had destroyed. If only she could see him as he really was—nothing, nothing!

He stumbled from the kitchen and onto the back porch. He crumbled to the floorboards and crouched there, huddled together as tight as he could, his arms locked around himself. He tried not to breathe, to shrink into the humid, close air.

Two hands seized him by the shoulders. A murmuring, distressed and confused, showered him. "What is it? What's the trouble? Tell me!"

He wrenched free and scrambled on all fours down the three steps to the ground. Somehow he got to his feet and then he ran until the crying of "Come back! Come back!" was blanked out.

Faster and faster he raced along the slick pavements, wanting to beat his head against the tree trunks as they passed him, wanting to leave bloody traces of himself behind until there was nothing left of him.

At last he slowed, his mouth wide, gasping in the rain until the scorch in his lungs subsided. He found he was in front of the brown, three-storied mansion, and as weary as the dying he entered the front hall and walked to the staircase.

A huge shape in black crashed into him. He fell.

"What you doing—spying on me?" It was Williston. "Say it! Admit you want to know where it is!"

Gravel tried to rise but was pushed back down.

"Say it, you scut!" He cuffed Gravel three times on the side of his head.

His ears ringing, Gravel tackled the giant around the knees and brought him to the floor. Williston raised both fists and was about to bring them down in a hammer-stroke when a voice as shrill as a whistle arrested the blow.

"What's going on here? Stop it this instant! Like a pack of wolves let loose."

The servant punched the boy in the stomach as they both got to their feet. Gravel's breath whooped out of him and he gagged.

"Stop it!" commanded Mr. Gant. "I'll turn you in for sure if you touch that boy again! I promise you—I'll turn you in for good! Twenty years in prison will calm your craziness!"

The old man guided Gravel into the library. "You come in, too," he instructed Williston. "I'm going to tell this boy what you are." He turned to Gravel, who was now seated on the edge of a straight chair. "He won't ever threaten you again. Be afraid to.

That's why I'm still whole." He was staring now at the stonelike figure of his servant. "Oh, don't imagine I haven't known your dreams of murdering me for my money. I may be a miser as they claim I am, but I'm no fool, not for one living instant."

Gravel glanced at Williston. The tall man's arms hung loosely at his sides, his back stooped, his face expressionless. He seemed numbed. For a flick of time there was something about this beaten man that echoed himself. Was this what he might one day become? He broke the thought in two and listened to Mr. Gant's cutting voice. "He killed his brother with a knife. I saw it. I was there. This was before my eyes went back on me. I was the only witness and I lied for him, gave him an alibi."

He paused to wipe off the spittle that flecked his chin.

"But why?" asked Gravel.

"So's I could own him. It's been a pleasant friendship, hasn't it?" he jeered at the seemingly non-attentive man before him. "He's completely obedient because he has to be, which makes him the perfect slave." He pointed at Williston. "Now get out!"

Just as the huge man turned to go Gravel caught such a rush of hate in his eyes his own skin tingled. How could either of them endure the other's presence? Or was Mr. Gant's enslavement as certain as Williston's?

The questions were still cluttering his mind when, an hour later, he took the dark journey up the three flights of stairs to his attic. He went on tiptoe, as though the slightest sound might call out the fearsome shape of the servant. He barricaded the door with the one chair and went to stand at the window. The night seemed doubly dense. There was no rain but also no stars to relieve the blackness.

A distant kind of thumping came from below. Was the hulk coming to get him, to stifle him slowly between his clapperlike hands? Why was he so afraid to be dead? He was dead already, divided into pieces and then put together again, his legs to cancel Mrs. Prior's lameness, his eyes Mr. Gant's, and his ears replacing Miss Ethel's. What did he care if the rest, the scraps, were pulverized? A web of self-loathing seeped into his fear as he watched the door being pushed open, the chair fall.

Williston was there.

CHAPTER

13

"Go on—kill me! Do it! Do it!" Gravel was nearing hysteria.

"Don't be an idiot." Williston's tones were like a cat's purr thrumming at him as the man stepped in, closing the door behind him. "I came to divide with you, that is if you'll help me."

"Help you do what?"

"No point in hating me. Not now. We can be on the same side." He chuckled liquidly. "There's profit in it."

"I don't know what you're talking about and I don't want to."

"You will."

"Then spit it out and go." Gravel had to force himself to defiance.

"We're going to get rid of the old man. Oh, don't look so surprised. He's ready to go, keeps saying he's ready. What if we shorten it by a few years? Might even be grateful—if we gave him the chance to say so."

Gravel wished he were big and strong enough to punch the grin from the man's face.

"You see, boy," he continued, "I can pay you."

"Pay? What are you talking about?"

"I found it. I found his hoard. It's buried beneath where the coal bin used to be. There might even be more than what I dug up but this is enough. I counted it. More than fifty thousand dollars for each of us. But it has to be right now." Williston's excitement had pitched his voice higher and higher until it could have been that of a fevered child.

Gravel shuddered.

"We'll plant him where his treasure was." He paused, waiting for Gravel to join his sick delight. But as he studied the white-faced impassivity of the boy his humor changed. Anger began to build in him. "You'll do it or—or I'll kill you too. One body more won't matter. You know about me now and you're either with me or nothing and my kind of nothing is a long time dead!"

He extended both arms, his thick fingers tensed to grab. Gravel ducked under them and leaped for the door. Before the giant could wheel about-face he was out on the landing. He plunged downward, not even conscious of falling twice in his desperation. He knew as he skidded across the last landing that he should somehow warn Mr. Gant, but all he could manage now was to flee the horror behind him.

Ten seconds later he was out and cutting through the night to anywhere. He ran until he couldn't. He flung himself on the ground and just breathed for a long while. Then, at last, he raised his head and looked around him.

The trunks of trees columned the dimness. The earth was wet from the rains and smelled pungently of leaf mold. He could smell, too, his own sweat, the acrid evidence of his fear. He listened. No sounds, no sounds at all, only the crackle of a few twigs as he raised himself up to a sitting position. Was there nothing alive in these woods, no birds, no small animals? Was even the wind absent from this tomblike forest?

He opened his lips to say something, anything, to disrupt the silence, then clamped them shut. There was a voice, but it came from inside him and the words were chanted. "So you left him alone. You left him alone. To be murdered, murdered, murdered." Gravel thrust his head between his legs, pressing against his ears. But the voice did not cease. "You're gutless. You're gutless. You care about nobody. You trust nobody. You love nobody. You're all shadow. You look like shadow. You act like shadow. You even smell like shadow."

A sudden rustling of leaves like finite, chittering agreements rose up around him. The boy clenched his fists and beat with his knuckles against his head until his skull ached, drumming away the leaf chatter.

Then in the middle of the darkness within his squeezed-down eyelids, he saw the image of Mr. Paynter bent over his drawing board, a brush fat with black paint in his right hand, slowly forming letters on whiteness. Gravel didn't want to read them but he had to. They were for him. One by one the words flowed from the brush. "I trust you to come back."

The image vanished and a second one replaced it. It was a tall, bony man, his mouth wide and moving as though calling for help, his arms waving like spindly branches. Gravel strained to clear the vision that was pronged so truly onto the wall of his mind. It was not Gant but his father. For an instant he stayed locked against the strange rise of hurting in his chest. Then he let it spread, through his ribs up to the base of his throat. He opened his eyes and the presence was gone. He scrabbled to his feet and ripped through the heavy night toward the brown mansion. It was too late for both of them, but he had to try.

When he reached the house, it was blanked out by darkness. No lights. Was Williston filling the space behind the front door? Would he crash down on him the moment he came into the hall? Gravel turned the doorknob as delicately as though he were resetting a clock. He pushed the door one inch forward, then two, then a foot, two feet. He went in sideways so that he faced the possible attack. Nobody. He crept to the library. No one. But the door leading to the basement was ajar.

His body went suddenly cold. Was the servant baiting him to come down and be beaten, be smashed by those terrible hands? Had he already killed Mr. Gant and would now be shoveling up the dirt to make a grave, a hole wide enough for two corpses?

Gravel rubbed his icy hands on his cheeks and flexed his fingers to decrease their numbness. He took a deep breath and began a long, crablike descent into the nightmare dark below. Still not even a whisk of sound. He remembered that Williston had said he had found the money in the room where the coal was. Was he waiting in there, a monstrous spider of a man, his great arms extended to crush him?

Gravel looked inside. The faint lightening of the blackness from the one window outlined an elongated shape on the floor, a shape so still it had to be dead. So the old man was gone. Shame like a sweep of fire flared up in him. He had known that he was to be assassinated and he had run away. He, too, was a murderer. Let Williston come now and break him, bone by bone, until he was finally out of it forever.

As if summoned, two arms bound him around the ribs. He didn't struggle or even turn his head. "God, make it fast," was his only thought.

Then the arms dropped away and a high cackling struck his ears. "Thought I was my old and faithful servant, did you? Thought old Gant was dead."

Gravel whirled to see the thin lips of Mr. Gant stretched to show his jagged teeth, his tongue waggling as he talked. "Come back to share the loot, did you, boy? Well, I fooled you both and now—oh, I've lovely plans for you now that Williston's been put out of the way. Lovely plans. Oh yes, I killed him. Had to after he had found my hiding place. Knew he would sooner or later so I was ready for him. Practiced going down those cellar stairs more than a hundred times. Had a gun loaded all these years. Wasn't hard to aim for the right place—knew his height—but I just wish I could have seen his face before I blew his head in!"

Gravel felt paralyzed, trapped in such rigidity he wondered if he were even breathing.

"Want to hear me tell your future, boy? Sure you do. Don't even need any cards to do it." He almost whined with pleasure. "You're going to be my servant now. Take Williston's place. Be nice to have something young in the house."

"But I did nothing," Gravel stammered.

"And you think you'll be believed after I testify that you killed my manservant? You think any jury would take the word of a stray who just came off the roads a few weeks ago? Not likely! We'll have a splendid time together, you doing exactly what I say, no matter what. Oh, you'll soon get used to it. After all, Williston did."

Suddenly Gravel felt his bondage almost as though he had been physically enclosed, round and round, with flat, steel bands. The edges of them cut into him, bled his mind of any desire but for freedom.

He faced the grotesque grinning of the mad old man. "I won't! I'm going and I'm not coming back. You won't tell your lies after I'm gone. You'll always be too afraid—not of my telling—afraid of losing your money."

The boy stepped back as Mr. Gant's arms flailed at him. Then the man's voice altered to a whine. "But I need you, boy. I'm an old man who's almost totally blind. I'll make it worth your trouble. I'll even pay you."

Gravel quickly left the room, the house. The first earliness of dawn was in the sky but he didn't see it. A light wind brushed coolness on his face but he didn't feel it. He was almost hollow now, but he still had two more things to do before he ended the masquerade, before he cut himself free of what he had become —an unreal being not fit to live.

CHAPTER

14

From Mrs. Prior's porch he watched the rising of the sun and wondered without really caring what it would be like to be a rock, as he had so long ago said to Mr. Paynter. Would the first morning layer of sun filter through the granite particles, or must it be noon before the stone would know the sun to be in the sky? He fastened his mind around these thoughts to keep the others at bay. He knew they would come at him soon enough.

He waited until he could hear the sounds of Mrs. Prior getting up, her weight upon the stairs, and then gave her time to go into the kitchen before he knocked.

"Come in!" she called.

Her eyes shone as she saw who it was. "But you've never come so early before, child! And you're tired, I can tell. Sit down. Pour yourself a cup of coffee when it's hot and I'll make you some toast. Even have a jar of strawberry jam that's never been opened."

He punched her chatter with "I've left the Gant house."

For one instant something about him seemed to startle her. There was a difference in him. Then, "For good? I'm glad. Time you got out from under that miserable man who never did a good thing in his life, that I'm sure of. But why? Hope there wasn't any unpleasantness for you."

Gravel felt his facial muscles jerk in a kind of spasm.

"Well, don't worry yourself, dear. Whatever it was will soon be forgotten. And now I can propose what I decided a while ago. You can settle in with me. Oh, it won't be hard on you. You'll have my son's room and you can fix it up any way you wish and you'll go to school just the way he did and come home and tell me all about who you talked to and what your teachers said and what games you won and I'll listen just as I used to, though he never talked much."

Gravel's attention drifted. Why couldn't she see that he wasn't her son, that it had only been an accident that those clothes were his size. Or was it just anybody she needed? Could any stranger, any young boy, have stitched up her loneliness? A thought thrust through him like a tiny arrow. Maybe she really loved him for himself just as he was. He shrugged that off. Not this Gravel Winter, the pretender, the play-actor who had treated her just as falsely as the dead person in all her photographs.

"—and you needn't worry that you'll not be doing your share," he picked up her talking, "because I'll let you help me just as you have been doing. Oh, we'll be cozy together, you'll see." She pushed herself up from the table and poured two cups of coffee. It was the first time Gravel had not served her.

"I can see you're depressed about something, but you just let it pass. That's how I managed when my son left me. Just let the days go by until I felt better. It's the only way."

Gravel took a swallow of coffee. It was so hot it hurt his mouth. That seemed to dissolve his silence. Why couldn't he give her what she asked of him? Deception would be a kindness.

He put down his cup and tentatively, hesitantly, put out his hand and touched hers. Her words halted as her eyes filled with tears that did not fall.

He spoke. "I have to leave you, Mrs. Prior."

She looked at him fully, and he knew she was finally seeing him. Then she nodded and blinked her eyes clear. "I saw it in your face, your own dear face," she said almost inaudibly. Her tone strengthened. "Is there anything I can give you to take with you? Anything at all? Money? Clothes? Whatever I have."

"I won't need anything," he said, almost adding "ever again" but suppressing it. He couldn't distress her further.

He got up and saw her prepare to follow. "No, don't," he said, keeping his voice gentle.

"I want to see you to the door."

He offered her his arm as she began to limp through the living room.

"No. I must manage for myself just as I used to before you came. I'll be fine. Don't you ever worry about that."

At that moment he realized that for whatever brief time he existed, he would in some entrenched corner of himself worry about her. He looked up at her from the sidewalk, just once, and watched her face as she said simply, "Goodbye, Gravel Winter," and he knew that what she was really telling him was all in her eyes.

He did not turn back.

CHAPTER

15

This time he went to the back door and looked in. Miss Ethel's house was so little he could see through the two of its three rooms. Next he tried the bedroom window, but no sign of her.

Then he heard the laughter. Was she hiding from him? Once more he scanned the kitchen. There she was on the floor playing with the kitten. The tiny animal was executing quick little pounces after the walnut tied onto a piece of string. Miss Ethel would let him capture it in both paws and then move it enticingly a few inches away. And her delight was twin to the kitten's.

Gravel was now standing behind her. Should he just go away? Why was he here? She would wonder for a while what had happened to him, where he had gone, but someday would forget he had ever passed by. But he knew this was not true. No matter what he was, what he had failed to be, she would not forget him. The burning behind his ribs that had begun in the forest returned.

Just then the cat saw him and leaped at one of his shoes, attacking it with soft swipes of its paws.

Miss Ethel looked up, then got to her feet. "What will you think of me?" she said, her voice still light with laughter. "That

I've turned childish? Well, I have, you know. This little creature is so full of fun it's contagious. But here I am babbling about myself and I'm so glad to see you!" She moved out of a shaft of sunlight to see him better. "But it's not afternoon yet! Not nearly. You've never come at this time before. Is anything the matter?"

She patted his arm with a touch as feathery as the kitten's.

He wanted to tell her to stop, to take her hand away. She might become infected, not knowing she was touching a shadow, an unreal being unhealthily joined and filled.

All joy had left her now and her eyes were grave. She turned him toward the back door and pushed him gently in front of her. "I must show you what happened in my garden after you went yesterday." She halted him in front of a rose bush. A single rose, red as an autumn apple, had bloomed. She drew a pair of scissors from her pocket and cut its stem. "I want this to be yours. Since my deafness—and that's most of my life—I've never had the chance to give very much. Not enough people to know and to love. And what few there were didn't really care. But you do. You've become all the friends I never had."

He had to stop her, to block this flow of affection that could never take root in the self he was. He bent his mouth to her ear. "You mustn't feel like that. I'm not worth it. I have to leave you."

Her face lost its openness and became strained. "Is that what you said?" she asked. "Did you say you had to leave me, or was it just my old ears making up a sadness? They do sometimes."

He shook his head. "No, it's true."

"But why? Oh, I thought something was the matter. I knew it the instant I saw you. But tell me why. Make it short so's not to tire yourself, but tell me."

"I can't. I don't know why myself." And before he could be really certain that her eyes held tears he swerved away from her, out of the house, across the back stoop. He saw that the kitten had followed him and he swiftly scooped it up and thrust it back into the kitchen.

He did not look back, but she saw him carefully put the rose into his jacket pocket.

CHAPTER
16

Again, as in the beginning, he walked the highway, asking nothing and once not even noticing when a car slowed to offer him a ride. He knew the way back but each step became harder to take. Would the terrible greyness be there waiting, waiting to swallow him up? If he were to destroy the patchpieces that he was, it had to be by his own will, not down a tunnel of madness.

But he had to finish it, and that meant a final farewell to Mr. Paynter. Hadn't he said, "I trust you to come back"? He could never right the charade he had played with Mrs. Prior and Miss Ethel. They had loved someone he wasn't, a kind of clown who had known his manners and how to please. But now the mask, the costume had to be stripped off. After Mr. Paynter. And for that reason he pushed against his fear with each mile, cleaving the thickness of it.

He had just come to the first scrubby street of the town when the sun went out. Clouds piled up like mountains covered the sky, charcoal clouds. He shivered. It would soon be raining. He told himself that the greyness above him was just sky, not a mirror of his feelings. A jagged pain shot through his skull. He forced his feet to move, hearing now the pounding of his heart in his ears. At last he found himself before the sign painter's door. He stopped.

If only the earth would split open, receive him into its jaws. He would fall and fall until he met the bottom and be finally crushed and out of it. And he could make it happen. But later, not just now, not until he finished the journey.

He knocked, hoping at this last second that Mr. Paynter wouldn't be there, or that he wouldn't hear, or that he was in bed and too tired to get up to answer. He would not knock twice.

"Come in! It's not locked!"

There he was, seated at his drawing board, a blank white carton before him. The man turned, looked long and steadily at him, and then said, "It's you. Come over here and tell me how to place the words. I've been in a puzzle over it all morning and it has to be finished today." He pulled up a stool and motioned Gravel to sit beside him.

Gravel wanted to yell at him, to screech out the sentences that battered like wasps in his brain. "You fool, don't you remember that I deserted you, that I walked out and didn't care whether or not you needed me? Don't you know that I sold myself to the first people who were seeking a prop, that I shaped myself to please them so they wouldn't know what I was? Don't you know yet what I am? Nothing! Nobody!" No sound came from his lips, but why was he, Gravel, remembering that inward image of his father that had changed his hate into pity? Why did he feel again the touch of his hand on Mrs. Prior's? And Miss Ethel's rose—why had he kept it, given it the shelter of his pocket?

Mr. Paynter's eyes were now looking into his as though he were listening, hearing what the silence said. Then the man smiled. "These are the words," he said. "A bit crazy for a shoe store but what they told me they required. 'Want to fly? Let our shoes do it.'"

Underneath these sentences Gravel was hearing the same voice coming through all the layers of greyness until the words were right with him, here in this room: *I trust you to come back. I trust you to come. I trust you.* He returned the man's look and faintly shaped the words with his own mouth, testing them.

A long moment later he sat down on the stool and suggested in tones that trembled just a little, "Why not place the words within a pair of wings?"

The man laughed and handed the boy his stick of charcoal. "Go ahead. You try it."

Born in Spokane, Washington, Julia Cunningham took to the road of many towns and schools from California to Virginia. Then, like most writers, came a variety of jobs—a music company, a museum, a movie magazine, a book store, among others. A year in France focused her love of language and what followed from her typewriter became her first published book. Since that time she has created for young readers many well-loved books including *Burnish Me Bright, Far in the Day, The Treasure is the Rose, Maybe a Mole,* and the widely acclaimed *Dorp Dead.* She enjoys living in the real and the imaginary world, whether writing or selling books, presently in Santa Barbara, California.